# MAGICAL SCIENCE

BY

MALCOLM DE CHAZAL

TRANSLATED BY JEAN BONNIN

Also by Jean Bonnin


Novels:

*A Certain Experience of the Impossible* (2009)

*Lines Within The Circle* (2012)

*The Cubist's House* (2015)

*One Eyed Fish* (2017)


Poetry, Aphorisms and Articles:

*Un-usual Muse-uals* (2012)

*Being and Somethingness* (2015)


Translations:

*Magical Sense* by Malcolm de Chazal (2015)

# Jean Bonnin

Jean Bonnin was born in Lavaur, in the Tarn in France;
he was brought up mainly in the United Kingdom. He took his first
degree in government and politics at Birmingham, and his second
in political philosophy at Hull; his doctoral research was
on the theories of despotism. After university he lived and
worked in France, Portugal, Ireland, and the former
East Germany. On deciding to leave the underground and
avant-garde music scenes of Berlin and northern France behind
him – but not to abandon his music-making altogether –
he returned to Wales where he now lives and writes in his
empty room looking out over the empty field which leads
to the empty town which is on the edge of the empty waters
which, if one is brave enough to attempt to cross, eventually
lead to the edge of something or other. And if one allows oneself
to be taken by the currents, plunging over into this unknown,
one will enter a magical world…

Magical Science
An Original Publication of Red Egg Publishing
An imprint of Red Egg International
First published in the UK by Red Egg Publishing
in 2016
www.redeggpublishing.com

British Library Cataloguing-in-Publication Data
A catalogue record for this book is available upon
request from the British Library

ISBN: 978-0-9571258-7-2
While every effort has been made to contact copyright-holders,
if an acknowledgement has been overlooked, please contact the publisher

# MAGICAL SCIENCE

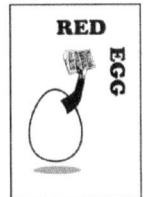

BY

MALCOLM DE CHAZAL

TRANSLATED BY JEAN BONNIN

# INTRODUCTION

Malcolm de Chazal was a poet, writer and artist who possessed an alchemical and transcendental quality which infiltrated both his work and his very essence.

The mystery which surrounds him, needless-to-say, is in no small part connected to his artwork and, moreover, to his writing. This is not the whole story, however. His relationship with the surrealist movement and its esotericism also plays its part, as does the self-imposed meditational and sequestered nature of his existence; an existence which enabled him to see and experience reality differently, possibly as it really is. Thereby, by his own admission, guiding him towards a completely unique approach to how to write.

 Each one of these various strands helps us to comprehend a little of the man behind the art and the writing that we call Chazalian. But possibly none more so than his intriguing family history and its connections with alchemy.

His family had been French land-owning aristocracy in the Auvergne and the Loiret. His ancestor the Earl François de Chazal de la Geneste along with Antoine

Toussaint de Chazal de Chamarel moved to the island of Mauritius during the Enlightenment. François was a Rosicrucian who, it is said, manufactured alchemical gold at will, and due to his visionary abilities predicted all of the events that were to take place during the French Revolution. Malcolm de Chazal stated that at one time he repeatedly kept feeling strong sensations as to the location of the burial tomb of his ancestor François. This was a very intriguing disclosure since, as he said himself, Rosicrucians must be certain that all evidence of them ever having existed must vanish upon their demise.

In a letter to André Breton in 1949 from Pastor René Agnel, Malcolm de Chazal is described as a "poet, explorer in cosmology and ethnology, expert in esotericism, heterodox, theologian, and independent militant [who] will remain until his dying breath an individual tormented by his quest of a truly liberated, and a truly purified spirituality, like Rimbaud, 'the man with soles of wind', in pursuit of the transformed life…"

In Magical Science de Chazal is creating a cosmology of the invisible whilst guiding us towards a methodology by which to interpret the pulses of the universe. Space reveals its secrets if we are open and willing to see them; and if, crucially, we are fortified with the definitions and identifications that can help us to prise open the plasticity of space and time.

Here Malcolm de Chazal is striving for the divine, striving to touch the brow of the all-seeing entity. The only way to do this, he believed, was to remove himself from the quotidian, enabling him to realise a meditative almost trance-like state.

As far as was possible he discarded reason in favour of the attainment of truth via the senses. He wished to eradicate the outside world so as to enable him to rebuild it both according to how he saw it and how he wanted it to be... thereby helping man to get closer to the divine essence of the universe.

Malcolm de Chazal's friendship with André Breton was longstanding; indeed he was included in Breton's list of surrealists. He was also highly regarded by Georges Braque who it was that first suggested he took up painting, and equally by Jean Dubuffet, the founder of Art Brut. All of these endorsements notwithstanding de Chazal nevertheless did not want to be solely categorised as a surrealist.

One of the reasons for this self-imposed remoteness was because he saw his work (certainly his written work) as deriving from the meditational and the spiritual rather than deriving from reason and the intellect. Of the Parisian intelligentsia, for example, he said their literature "is... far too literary. The people are too intelligent without being sensitive enough. The writers dazzle without moving you much."

Hence, it could be argued that de Chazal found a way to caress onto the page the beautiful connections and insights he experienced rather than think them onto the sheet of paper via the end of a nib, as is de rigueur. To de Chazal's mind, then, intellectualising restricts, whereas sensing through instinct, emotion and intuition opens the windows onto a life beyond the surface of all things.

# Malcolm de Chazal

Malcolm de Chazal (1902-1981) – was born in Mauritius to French parents... To begin with he was a writer and a poet. His most notable books being: Sens Plastique and Sens Magique... W.H. Auden said of him that he was "...the most original and interesting French writer to emerge since the war." And André Breton hailed him as a surrealist.

In 1950, at the suggestion of Georges Braque, he began to paint... Better known in the French-speaking world – as an influential artist who stands alone in both his approach and his style – he is now becoming appreciated in the English-speaking world as a free-thinker who is deserving of his place in art history.

He was seen as a surrealist, a mystic and an alchemist... Occasionally one glimpses similarities between his artwork and Van Gogh's, Matisse's and Derain's. His art has been described as post-modernist expressionism. To my mind he should be defined as a post-Fauvist. And if that is what he was, then he was the essence of what that approach was supposed to embody in its purest form: an animalistic and feral interpretation of the world through bold colours, harnessing the emotions whilst rejecting a rigid representational approach to art and the world...

Here, Malcolm de Chazal is offering us a glimpse of a key to a multiple padlocked door. And in so doing is revealing something of an inner and outer universe, to help us to begin to unlock the tightly bound answers to the questions that some of us spend our existences considering.

This is… Magical Science.

# MAGICAL SCIENCE

# MAGICAL SCIENCE

## SPACE

It isn't the same time in New York as it is in Tokyo. It isn't the same time in Paris as it is in Chandernagor. It isn't the same time in Moscow as it is in Buenos Aires.
And yet! …
The shadow beneath the tree at midday (the shadow being the 'small night'), the sun at its zenith, can be seen as the 'expansive night' of the antipodes, the midnight of nadir.
For it is but one and the same night, a seamless dress.
Midday and midnight reconciling, both identifying with *immediate time*.
What is 'immediate time'?
It is space, the seamless dress.

# INVISIBLE

If light could be seen, it is the only thing we would see. And it would be like a wall before our eyes, as opaque as the darkest of nights.
And no image would reach us.
Light is visible-invisible.
The invisible is the night in daytime, the colourless entity, enabling images to be transported to us by the light.
It is space that allows all to pass.
The light of day is a sleepless night.
So night continues, from the invisible to shadow to that which is colourless.


# ABSOLUTE NIGHT

It is never completely night for in this respect space can never be singled out. And the centre of the earth is on fire.
And the height of the night is crossed by stars.
Absolute night is unthinkable.


# THE MOON

The 'milk' of the sun is white.
The sun, having decanted its 'milk', becomes moonlight, that which gives the night its transparency.
Night in the fullness of day is wakeful reverie. Bathed in moonlight the night sleeps.

## DARKNESS

Darkness is the body drowned of 'milk'.
Darkness quaffs the light.


## THE MIRROR

It is the opaqueness and transparency that collide.


## THE ANTIPODES

Night has neither height nor depth, right nor left, beginning or end.
At either end of the antipodes, Man has neither his head in the clouds, nor in the sand; he remains upright in space. Space is always upright, whichever way it is turned. For *within* space everything rests.


## THE EYE OF THE NIGHT

Zeno failed to see with the night's eye.
Otherwise he would have seen that the bird **that** flies doesn't move.


## THE MOVING MOUNTAIN

Observe the cloud that runs along the **mountain crest**. Then suddenly, conversely, you see that it is the mountain moving. That which has 'moved' is yourself.

## THE SOUL

New York is far away from Mauritius.
**I name the distance**.
It used to take three months by sailing boat. These days,
by plane, it takes three days. An atomic aeroplane would
take us there in three hours and a rocket in three minutes.
The radio's even better, it can take us there in a third of a
second.
The day will come when nuclear television whisks us
there in a thousandth of a second.
We're moving rapidly towards the speed of instantaneous
time when we will attain the speed of space.
Do you want to go faster than the speed of instantaneous
time? Be on the plane of the soul.


## PHANTOMS

In between this lamp and the wall I pass my hand so as to
release and contort strange forms.
What are these forms? They are pre-objects.


## THE HYBRID

A man seated, ghostlike, without a man. His back is that
of the chair, his arms are rests and his behind is on the
seat.
This 'man' is somewhere between four feet and legs.
I have called him armchair.

## MUTATION

Fin, wing, front leg being the same 'arm'.
The whale is a re-adapted 'arm'.
Fish becomes bird and bird becomes fish.
Arms below, arms above are the components.

## THE ANGEL

One who has risen above his shadow is an angel.

## REVERSABILITY

The terrestrial globe is round time.
The horizon has never escaped the horizon.

## SUPPORT

The domed sky is to prevent the stars from falling on us.

## ANTECEDENCE

As far as night was concerned, the day had never begun.
Before darkness was; light is.

## MIME

The photograph is the shadow.
Cinema is the moving shadow.
Cinema in colour is the movement of reflection.
Radio is the echo.
Mix it all together like a mirage and you have television.
Man, to imitate will always be your raison d'être.

## FACE TO FACE

The superiority of the monkey over man is that the
monkey sees itself as a monkey in the mirror.

## MULTI-UBIQUITY

At crossroads space becomes human.
At all roundabouts there is a diminution in man's
conscience.

## LIGHT LOOSES ITS FOOTING

Space is unsteady in its two tone dress.

## CUBISM

The art of butchering space.
Picasso is not a painter but an anatomist.

## THE ALPHABET

The periodic table of words.


## CORRESPONDANCE

Her voice matched her face which resembled a bird.


## INSTINCT

Horses like carrots; do you know why?
It is because the horse is a nasal-creature, and the carrot is
a nasal-vegetable.


## THE SCARECROW

Attached to the ground, a bulging belly, frayed collar and
the head stuffed with a cork, like a hat.
This 'gentleman' is the bottle.
The man-bottle is the man who did this and is frightened
of his own shadow, the inventor of himself.


## THE DUCK AND THE WATER

His every gesture is paddling, and his voice cries out as
the water makes ducks.

## FALSE TEETH

The toothless cock approaches the grain of corn in order to wear solar false teeth.


## HYPOCHONDRIAC

The steam pipe always has a cold, the exhaust pipe is still coughing, the engine has ataxia, perpetual locomotive.
The machine has hiccups, spits, vomits.
The Factory is a hospital of screams, where all the bodies are in strait jackets.
The laboratory, the fools in charge.


## THE LIVING EARTH

The heart of the earth pulses, blood is the magnetism and the diastolic and systolic are worked by the poles.
The mountains rise-up and fall in the diurnal-nocturnal cycles, the Earth breathes and we are part of its own life.


## THE EXPANSE

Space pulsates, breathes, in the diastolic and systolic of reverse, and the blood in motion is by my side as I advance from pole to pole within perspective.
I stop , everything stops.
I move, everything moves.
Such is the 'trick' of perspective.

Recall the shadow that pulsates and breathes in both directions, along with the circulating day.

And think of the tide of seasons, the tide of the seas, the tide of sap, the tide of wheat.

As with shadow, space moves with you and yet is nevertheless static. Static movement gives a sense of place, of living order.

# INTERPENETRATION

A house was constructed for her to the measurements of her body, roof for the head, eye open at the level of the skylight, a bosom as full as the body of her home, the fountain of her hips as solid as her basement.

She climbed the stairs within herself with gestures mirroring her stairs.

And her legs descended with the large steps of her hairless limbs.

She could welcome you to her home from a long way off. Her skylight eye would give you the signal.

# MOMENTUM

The lily trampled the shadow to go in front of the light.

# THE ABSOLUTE

*Water swims*
It is not water that moves, but its word.

## THE FIRE OF LOVE

In the sun there are flowers that do not burn.
For they themselves are light.


## FIRE

Night cannot burn and the sun is without ash.
Ash is the planet.


## THE WALKING EARTH

The shoes of shade, it is the earth.


## UNALTERABLE

Only God can shift the night.


## THE BOOK OF LIFE

With the fingers of flowers around me, I turn the leaves
of my soul-album.
And I am in the garden of God.

## SLEEP DURING THE DAY

He chased his shadow and caught it when the night came.
This was the essence of his dreams.
Thus time passes for many.

## WINTERING

The tree rooted itself in the air when winter came, and life
was infused into the branches of its roots.

## NEITHER HOT NOR COLD

Shade is cool in summer and hot in the winter.

## NEITHER LARGE NOR SMALL

From both ends the telescope was able to see that it was
unable to measure itself.
It could see both ends of space.

## KNOWLEDGE

Only when the tree stopped moving did the breeze
become conscious of itself. And hence the tree becomes
the breeze.

## UNCONSCIOUSNESS

Sensual pleasure was frightened.
Man was thinking about it.


## TRANSLUCID

This transparency harbours the darkest night.


## THE PSEUDO PAINTER

The painter cooked his colours and then ate them.
He should have eaten them first.


## THE PSEUDO SCULPTOR

The man was marble.


## THE TRUE MUSICIAN

His gestures were musical.


## THE GENUINE POET

He had words behind him and the Word in front.

## THE INSPIRED

He only knew he had spoken when the eye opposite returned his echo.

## THE TRUE WOMAN

The man in her.

## THE TRUE MAN

Beyond woman.

## GOD

That which is more than ourselves without ceasing to be us.

## THE UNIVERSE

Man opened up and fanned out.

## HEAVEN

Our pure Word.

## HELL

Our refusal to express ourselves.

## LIFE

Everything and the others too.

## SOCIETY

Everything one could want, except the men.

## GEOMETRY

A clear profile hidden in the shadows.

## THE NUMBER

To count from one to infinity, without even arriving at the end of one – an act of folly.

## CHARM

To constantly change whilst remaining the same.

## THE BIBLE

A book that defines us which has no significance.


## JESUS CHRIST

A man who completely discovered the meaning of life; the POET.


## JOHN THE BAPTIST

The man who knew the man who completely discovered the meaning of life.


## JUDAS

A man of science, a philosopher, the sage, the theologian, the literati, all intelligent men.


## A PEARL OYSTER

A pearled butterfly fallen from the sky.


## THE PEARL

A moon sun in the rain.

## SAINT PETER

A pope who ended up a poet.

## DEATH

A change of mood, a door to space.

## THE DOUBLE RAINBOW

Two colourful shapes facing the light with their backs to the night.
'Arc upon the clouds', the ark, the sign of man.

## PHASES OF THE MOON

A spinning head.

## THE HEAD

A seated body.

## THE BODY

An upright face.

## THE COMET

A failing sun. Neither ash nor smoke.

## MOSES

He who speaks of Jesus in the form of a Temple.

## JESUS

He who created Moses.

## THE LAMB

Jesus created from the sun.

## MARY MAGDALENE

The anti-nun.

## PILATE

All Christians, the bourgeois face.

## THE CROSS

The many lined ledger.

## THE FAIRY

God.

## LITTLE DWARVES

Angels.

## THE COLOURS OF THE SUN

The blue blues. The yellow yellows. The green greens. The red reddens.

## THE LOOK IN THE EYE

The earthly vision.

## THE EYE IN THE GAZE

The celestial vision.

## NOAH'S ARK

The sun on the waters of night.

# THE EYELID OF THE SUN

The night. It is raised for evermore.

# THE ECLIPSE

The eyelid of the night.

# THE MYTHICAL TRINITY

The free faced mirror. Narcissus in its entirety.

# THE MYSTIC

He who wishes to read the book of light without turning the pages of colour.

# THE TWO DEFINITIONS OF DOWNFALL

Man descends to animal, animal descends to vegetable, vegetable descends to mineral. Evolution is a decompression.
Evolution has stopped, man has surpassed himself, taking the horse in the car, the beef in the locomotive, the eagle in the aeroplane, the shark in the submarine and throwing himself into his mechanical double which is the robotic future of man, *Evolution* overtaken.

## BREATH TRAINING

Our DOUBLE gasps but does not breathe. When finally it breathes we will be on the 'other-side'.

## FLYING SAUCERS

'Apparitions'. Profane miracles of Science controlled by the atomic church.

## RELATIVITY

The fish has to believe that the bird is beneath the water.

# THE WORD

Professor Albert Einstein, on announcing his THEORY OF RELATIVITY, knowing that the theory was based on an indefinable premise, was unable to encapsulate anything had, by force or choice, to define his Theory of Relativity as a constant.

This constant, assuming its constant, is the speed of light.

This leads to a *Geo-centricity of Light* and clearly shows the impossibility for man to embrace the universe, *from the point of view of the universe,* to come out of himself to see life from the point of the whole and not from the part.

Derived from this impossible synthesis is the idea of total emptiness, which is the *space of separation.*

And science defines itself through the principal of *divide and know*, which in essence is its problem.

Under the scalpel of anatomical science, thus, the Universe will not give itself away.

Yet, the Universe is not in a vacuum.

And the constant assumed by Einstein, that is to say the uniform speed of light, defines the movement of light in the void.

Let us confront the meaning of 'speed' to reduce the sense of emptiness.

Real space, that which we are presented with according to our perspective, develops more and more of a plastic feel as we get to the heart of perspective (all opens and closes in two reversing gestures, and there is some kind of incessant plastic swirling by our sides), but a constant remains at the heart of this eternal space spasm, the constant being from the sense of proportion, which does not move.

Thus at the heart of that which moves is immobility.

*Immobile palpitations* are space, *palpitating immobility*, pure paradox and magic. For space is magic and not physical.

This spasm allows for all life in all of space's dimensions. And the proportional constant guarantees a sense of place.

But *immobile palpitation* is an absolute. And therein lies the crime of science to have created in the heart of magic a dividing act.

Isolating the constant, putting the proportional aside, evolves the sense of *precision,* and life defined in the measure of metre, the proportional code, here is the sense of distance. And with the ticking of the clock, defined within the precision of time and referring to the measure of distance, is the meaning of 'speed' and defines movement in emptiness.

The speed of light assumed as a constant is the concept of light travelling in emptiness.[1]

What this doesn't convey is the magical sense of movement at the centre of this magical world. Nonetheless, let us continue.

Having isolated the constant that is proportionality, to give us a greater sense of precision, the state of plasticity is separated. And from the spasm that consists of concave and convex undulations, halted and disassociated, the sense of plasticity is entombed within a transparent glass box which serves as a lens. And the microscope and the telescope have evolved into tools that can take a microcosmic and macrocosmic stock list of space (which for us represents the undulating spasms of either end of infinity).

The division infused into the centre of this magical environment means that PHYSICS has evolved.

And science, with its fixed measures, leads the Universe to sclerosis.
The error, therefore, would be to create a life full of movement in the void, thereby banishing any sense of real movement and real environment.

---

[1] Out of this concept is born the absurdity of the star which has already died millions of years ago whilst nevertheless its light continues to reach out in the emptiness of space. And it is in the makeup of man from which one would have taken away all the worthlessness he is expected to contain and which would typify vacantness as a particle visible only under the microscope, therefore reducing man to human atom.

Consequently science can be nothing more than formulary, a philosophy of numbers, arguments with accompanying statistics, everything encapsulated within the auspices of a geometry that leaves only the analysis of angles behind, representing a physical world where the number zero is obsolete, where the circle is the vertigo of void, where the idea of the point and the centre constitute this state of inertia, where the code of algebraic symbolism is the pursuit of colours at the fulcrum of chaos, and where with staccato movements the mechanical motor function of mathematics injects epileptic gesture into the mix.

Thus through the Revelation of Magical Space, all is restored.

Instead of the 'speed' of light in the void, it is the movement of light at the centre of the night, the night here to mean space, true space, sprawling, all engulfing magical space. And hence the Sense of Emptiness is concerned with the idea of *Discontinuity*, that which eternally divorces life from existence, the Magical Space known as CONTINUITY.

And the identification of space with the night in the sense of CONTINUITY (Space which gathers and enables the infinite differentiation of all within its centre), this identification of Space with the Night in the sense of CONTINUITY is named by shadow which, progressing with the moving object, is none other than the night which did not leave itself and continues, everywhere and always, in all directions for ever. THE SIGN OF SHADOWS, here being the *indicative of the movement of light,* shadows presenting the ever present night, which everywhere and always presents itself.

And the invisible night is also the invisible space, space which is not often seen at the heart of light, space here being without colour, the absence of colour which identifies with the invisibility of shadow, and is forever and always the night.

But the Sign of Shadows will truly reveal its supreme sense, when we reveal its *ambivalence*.

In one sense shadow defines the magical realm its spasm reveals (the shadow being an immobile pulsation) and in another sense shadow reveals, through its visual lining, the movement of light as a perpetual adaptation of its, and all, images, consequently signifying by its sign the LINK between image and light, their intimate union and their indissolubility.

Thus SHADOW becomes the key which opens, by its ambivalence, both the doors of light and the meaning of the night.

And the SHADOW is a sign of *physical matter*, the SHADOW unequivocally reveals to us in a Lesson of all Things alchemical to do with movement what exactly is the magical worth of matter, which sadly we have dragged into the physical world.

But there is one type of movement which manages to escape the laws of space.

Let us talk about the *movement* of the soul. But it is the idea of the soul defined in a new way, its true way - a way that considers the SOLAR STATE of man (the place that night never reaches and consequently the place where life exists beyond space).

It should be stated straight away, the soul is to do with CHARM, the way to access the meaning of GLORIOUS STATE, and which is the essence of light and the essence beyond the night.

Here we are struck by a necessary digression.

We have mistakenly taken the soul to mean *double*.

The *double* is still no more than the fundamental state of our terrestrial existence, unburdened of its hereditary nature and taken as the *voluntary body*.
This voluntary body is the amorphous body we assume after our death. And they that do not access the meaning of the soul, which is the GLORIOUS STATE, will remain in their *double* forever.

The digression we are making enables us to distinguish between the *double,* the amorphous body, and the soul, the glorious body. One is tied to time and space. The other outside of time and space. One is dependent on its position. The other is outside and beyond all positions depending uniquely on a world of states.

The DOUBLE, amorphous body, is nothing more than an envelope for the soul.

Our terrestrial life aims at understanding our soul, *via* the amorphous double.

And the soul pierces our terrestrial visage, *via* the DOUBLE, through the body of power that we call CHARM.

Charm is a magical state that is constantly renewing itself.

Those who have found their souls appear to be perpetually ageless and rejuvenated. Eternity seems to exist within them. They appear to be as on their first day and they have the mark of childhood on their faces and all their being is filled, and this is the state of naivety which is the sign of innocence.

Their unlimited power to rejuvenate makes their word infinite. And the all, named in simplicity, at the heart of nakedness (the soul is the naked sense of light never attained by the night). Their *amorphous double* makes them healers and their solar power confers a state of peace to their presence.

Their perpetual renewal dispels the world weariness from their presence. They reveal themselves as a body of joy. Such is the child whose charm is irresistible.

Supporting the MAGICAL REALM in its final throes, we have the impulses of the soul.

Let the terrestrial be eclipsed and the fundamental outer casing be rejected by death and here is the DOUBLE in its amorphous beauty, in its gown of light, the last envelopment of THE BODY OF GLORY. And this is the final transformation prior to reaching the State of Splendour.

This is the ultimate soaring ascent.

And this feeling of ascension, of being winged, is the feeling of the soul forcing its way through into daily life. The manifestation of the soul, there, right in front of us.

It is the painter who is applying the subtlest of strokes to give a sense of the infinite. It is the sculptor who surpasses the marble he is working on to reach a state of oneness with the spirit. It is the note played by the musician which contains within it the sound of eternity.

And it is the simple being who has such 'angelic' expression, projects life to beyond the everyday life and bestows a charm in the eyes that reflects a sense of the infinite.

The shortcut to God is the state of the soul known as *The Realm of Ultimate States.*

The expression of being here is the countryside passing before the eyes of an angel.

Over and above words is the immediate word.

And the Word here is all life. It is the sense of god which expresses itself as conscience-universe, seen in stretches of countryside, in magical gardens.

The SYMBOL gives us the sense of divine nature in the word.

Here permeating amongst us, at the heart of our terrestrial life, is a narcissus grove and a bouquet of roses. Certain beautiful things are and remain just that, namely Beautiful, and never reach a higher plane.

But seen through the prism of what has essential meaning, via the world of symbols, the narcissus filled field and the rose filled grove are CONDITIONS OF THE SOUL.

That is to say, here, that man unanimously labels the sentiment of his life in the DIVINE ORDER OF THE WORD.

Thus terrestrial life is a School of the Heavens, where man becomes CONSCIOUS of his soul and ultimately the meaning of life; man does it through his work which is his life.

Outside of any utilitarian idea, the terrestrial image turns the pages of the album of the soul, an album of allegories and the book of life.

And Man, understanding his soul here below, ultimately transported into the realm of symbols and revived with the sun within, ASCENDS.

The TASK here below is to let go, to give oneself. Treasures shine in the depths of the being with the GIFT. These treasures are the treasures of Heaven, they concern the soul.

The TASK is to love, but to love through the free gift.

And the soul knows itself through the TASK.

*

And it is man taking responsibility for himself.

Man is in possession of these five senses including the Sense of Pleasure, SENSE OF PLEASURE which pivots the five senses making them get together and ultimately crowns and glorifies them.

And the pleasure is THE SENSE OF FIRE.

Solar pleasure is the Joy of Heaven. To be baptized with FIRE is to re-find one's soul.

Thus man who rejects his soul rejects charm, becomes impotent, committing the crime of Pleasure, and is fighting against the FIRE.

And this Fire within him becomes infernal.

Desire then remains grounded on earth.

And man is conversant neither in that which cannot be categorized nor in the cycle of continued rejuvenation.

In attempting to replicate the charm of the soul, man will move into the realm of fascination, using his impure *double*. And Fire alone will serve as a CONSTRAINT.

And this FIRE will become like GEHENNA (an inferno of jealousy and sensual delight), and only advances in order to devour.

Or it will be mystical Joy, enshrouded delight, revealed in the mirror-like surface of the LAKE OF FIRE, (Apocalypse), which can be thought of as Frozen Love.

These two forms of fire are unified within the idea of the SERPENT, which serves as an allegory representing the union of BURNING and FROZEN, the result being HELL.

Hell, here is excess in two meanings, denying the sense of the child, and the presence which invades or absorbs denies the other of his liberty, while the LIVING CHARM delivers us, provokes us, revives us, helps us to find ourselves.

CHARM, is the sense of the COMMANDMENT OF LOVE in man, and defines his creative power, that of renewal.

Animals live by their wits alone. They have no RESPONSIBILITY. They are directed by their instincts, and obey them.

Plants exist in their state of vegetal instinct, as rocks are in their own instinct. Elements follow their 'inclinations'.

Whereas man lives within a realm that supersedes mere instinct. And this is the *instinct of heaven* or The World Manifested in the Spirit.

And in the SYMBOLIC WORLD or THE HEAVEN OF LIFE, the bird is not completely a bird even though it presents itself as thus, the lily is not completely a lily though it presents itself as thus, the mountain is not completely a mountain even though it presents itself as thus, the elements are not completely elements even though they present themselves as thus. And life is not the complete manifestation of life even though it presents itself as thus, but is the manifestation of life above life.

The lamb is revealed within this life above life, but the terrestrial lamb is not present, the rose is present, but it is not the terrestrial rose that is present, the precious stone is present but it is not the precious stone within the terrestrial order that is present. The elements reveal themselves but not the elements we are accustomed to on earth. All reveals itself as if of this earth yet is not of this earth, everything exists in SPIRIT FORM and has a CELESTIAL sense.

AND THESE CELESTIAL ENTITIES ARE THE WORD IN ITS PUREST FORMS.

Thus the creative power in man becomes ultimately the creative power in the divine.

And the man who denies his soul deprives himself of this divine power, thus renouncing the part of him that is god.

And it is JUDAS, who betrays himself.
What does JUDAS do? JUDAS renounces himself.

However, the fact that man in his role as man epitomises the UNIVERSE, and in denying his soul, whilst being unable to reach for a UNIVERSAL sense within the Spirit, man by his proper creation, could create a CONSTRUCTED UNIVERSE, and in every sense this is the ARTIFICIAL WORLD at the hands of man, which will be the WORK OF IMITATION.

Unable to renew himself, man will move on from one task to another, and onto the essence of pure mimicry.

And it is the zinc swallow that is the aeroplane, the mime of the bird. And the zinc swallows will be mass produced in the factories.

Moving on to works of fascination, man will create bodies of illusion that are photos, television, radio and cinema.

And all of this will be through act of division and the body of scission will be brought under false synthesis.

And as far as the real world is concerned, man will be completely superseded by artificiality.

And from the sense of the infant, man will give in childishness, comic and cruel games, concerning all the works of INTELLIGENCE, illusory and menacing bodies.

And *intelligence* is the sense of the RASCAL tricking himself, whilst tricking others.

And it is the sense of the hoaxer and the liar, of the magician and the dog, of the idolater and the immodest, of the coward above all who, betraying himself, betrays all and renouncing himself becomes waylaid. And being lost he wishes to loose others, relishing in the pleasure of betrayal and loss.

Above all the rascal is the man of FABLES.

Having lost the WORD he has lost the sense of REALITY.

And the sum of his Invention, he, the man who exists outside of life, will be to invent a God who should and could be at his level in the alignment of his fable.

And there will be as many God(s) of the Fables as there will be possibilities of invention. And there will be as many God(s) as groups of men inscribed in their particular Fable.

And God who must unite will be equally he that divides man, man having lost his soul, and unable to rediscover the sense of the Living God.

Henceforth the word God reveals itself as the shallowest of words, a heartless word which resumes emptiness, the word God in its empty word leading to nothing but the domination of man by man, man cursing man mutually and making the word GOD a spiritual arm to put down one's neighbour, and making this word the tool of Human Discord.

Looking for the Harmonizer, the poet, finding the sense of infancy called the NAKED GOD, which is the light over and above the night, a Name of Man, Man being the Magical Sign of everything.

And the Night in its Plastic Body reveals itself as the FREE WILL, enabling the sense of CHOICE. And God freely calling the life to oneself, man can refuse IT and, by doing this, remains in the night and gives allegiance to eternal time and, accepting it, man leaves time and is the MASTER OF LIFE.

The Night explains thus, both the destiny of God (through the overwhelmed night) and the full and entire liberty for man to refuse his destiny; hell where man sits is the actual body of his refusal.

And God leaves this anathema to present himself as the God of Justice. And he that curses himself is none other than man himself, God, as the Called One or He Who Calls, being the ETERNAL SANCTIFIER.

And this *Perpetual and Incessant Call* which is Providence takes from man all rights to an alibi.

The meaning of life is here.

The animal is created, the plant is created, the stone is created, the elements are created. And man is created, and all here beneath is reproduced.

But all, except Man, is *uniquely* in the law of instinct and in the natural order.

For it is man, also in the laws of instinct and in the natural order, who is in addition and above all the being who is CALLED.

Man called is thus responsible.

And it is this responsibility that will ultimately judge him, from this IMMINENT JUSTICE which is the Law of Love. And it depends on us to reply to this Calling of Infinite Love.

And the destruction of the Earth comes from man himself, pawn of the Cosmic command to which Nature replies, humanity as a falling whole brings about the Fall of Nature in its entirety.

It is up to man, once more, to bring the sense of the Garden to the earth.

Finally, all depends on Man, because Man is the sign and the seal of life.

# NOTES AND ACKNOWLEDGEMENTS

Magical Science was mainly translated in Majorca and Wales, with final corrections and rewording undertaken in France. This was all done during the winter and summer of 2014-15.

I wish to express my gratitude to both Yvelaine Armstrong and the Fondation de Malcolm de Chazal for on the one hand asking me to translate Monsieur de Chazal's work in the first place, and, thereafter, for the support and encouragement I received.
	My thanks also goes to Finn Anson for all of his very much appreciated and invaluable help.

It is recommended that readers also consider reading the translation of Malcolm de Chazal's *Sens Magique*: Magical Sense. Also published by Red Egg Publishing.

Narberth,
Pembrokeshire, Wales.
15th January 2016

V1

www.redeggpublishing.com

www.ingramcontent.com/pod-product-compliance
Lightning Source LLC
Chambersburg PA
CBHW071317200626
46813CB00015B/2245